The Bookseller of Timbuktu

Written by John Parsons
Illustrated by Vasja Koman

Contents

NELSON
CENGAGE Learning™
For learning solutions, visit **cengage.com.au**

Meet the Characters

Kella

A wise bookseller.

Durar

Kella's daughter.

Souma

Kella's uncle.

Hasan Khalif

A kindly scholar.

Ahmed

A travelling bookseller.

Zaheen

Ahmed's son.

Dear Reader

When I started writing this story, I must tell you it was about something else. But as I wrote, Kella, the main character, became stronger and stronger, and somehow, she made me change my original manuscript to tell her story instead. She is a very persuasive woman, as you will discover in the following pages!

John Parsons
Author

Timbuktu

1. Timbuktu
2. The river Niger
3. The Sahara Desert
4. The rainforest
5. Modern-day Mali

1 The Heart of the World

For some people, when you say "Timbuktu", their imagination conjures up a dreamy picture of a mysterious place at the end of the world. That image is not true. I call Timbuktu home, and I can tell you that we are not at the end of the world. We are at its heart.

As I sit here, watching Ismail pore over the brittle pages of the scholarly book I have brought him, I can tell from his face we are both thinking the same thing. While I want the gold he keeps hidden within his robes, he wants the knowledge that the pages of my book promise to impart. Both of us wonder what can be half as precious as the things we wish from the other?

Ismail looks up from his pages and smiles. I know the bargaining is about to begin. Whoever speaks first will give away their position. I stare into Ismail's eyes and stay silent. Before he even begins, Ismail knows he is defeated. There are three *madrasahs*, or schools, which compete to be the centres of enlightenment in our city. Djinguereber, Sidi Yahya and Sankore. There is only one book. I have the upper hand.

"Fifty ducats, Kella," he says finally.

"One hundred and fifty," I reply without blinking.

"Eighty," he sighs. "And not one more."

There is a soft knock at the door and my daughter, Durar, enters.

"Mother, I know you do not wish to be disturbed, but el-Shabeni from Sidi Yahya is waiting outside. He says he is anxious for an audience with you."

A look of consternation passes over Ismail's brow. He strokes the page of the book before him, as if it were a stray kitten imploring him to find it a good home.

"One hundred and forty," he says, failing to disguise the tone of desperation in his voice.

I nod at Ismail. The deal is done. Eager to leave with his treasure, he burrows deep within his robes, his fingers searching for his purse.

"Tell el-Shabeni I have nothing for him," I order Durar. She leaves without a word, drawing the door silently behind her.

Ismail counts out his gold in fourteen small towers of ten ducats. I take my time to recount it once he has finished. Finally we stand and, without a word, bow our heads to each other.

After he leaves, clutching his precious volume, Durar reappears in my office.

"Perfect timing," I murmur, without glancing up.

"Mother, you should not trick Ismail like that. That poor man."

I look up at my daughter and smile.

"He is not a poor man, Durar," I say gently. "In Ismail's eyes, he has left richer than when he arrived at our door. In my eyes, we are also richer than when he arrived. What better bargain can be struck?"

Durar nodded. "That much is true. But el-Shabeni was not here," she said.

"He will be tomorrow," I said. "And I will make him wealthier and happier, too."

Here, at the very heart of the world, this is how our wealth and our contentment grow.

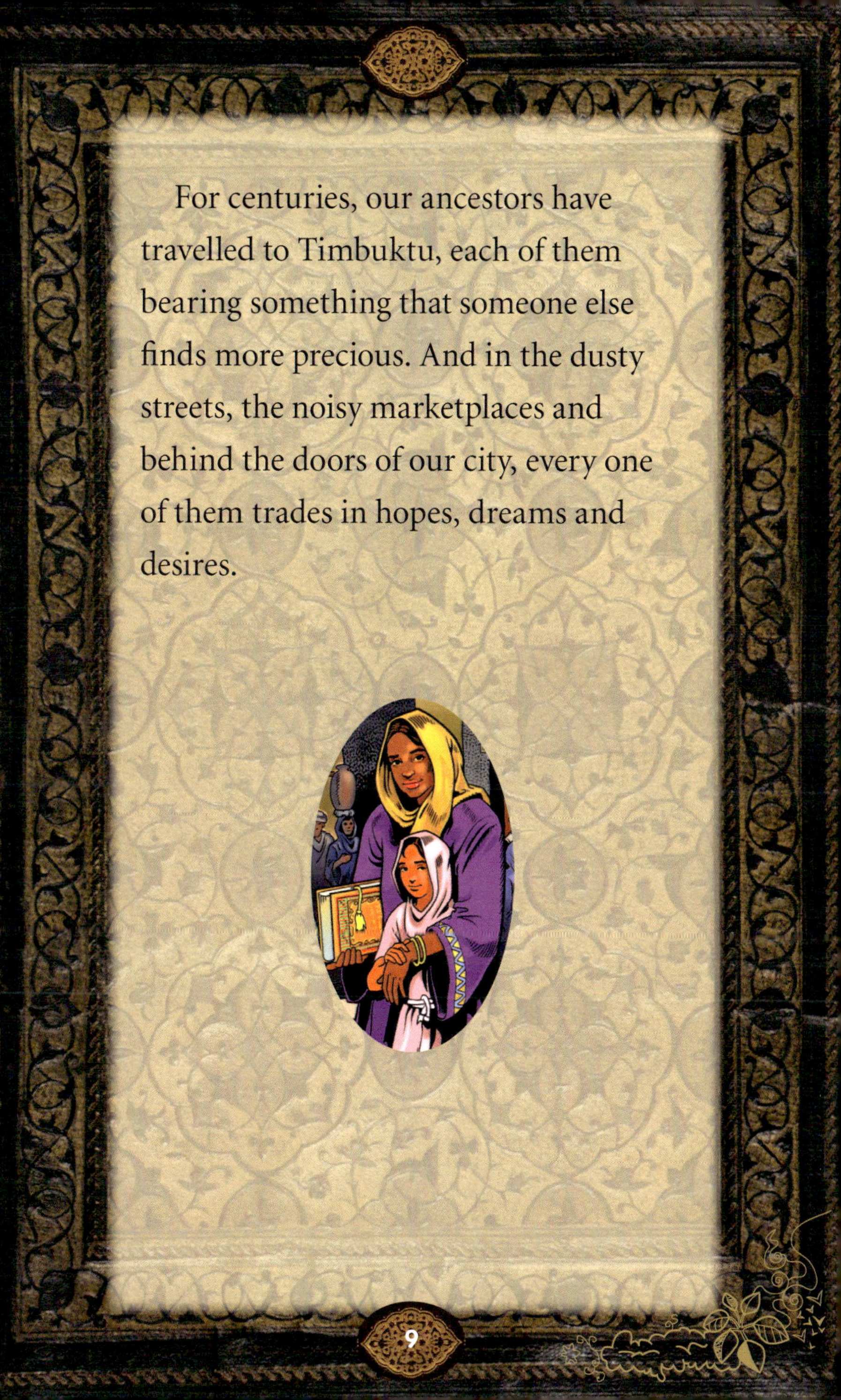

For centuries, our ancestors have travelled to Timbuktu, each of them bearing something that someone else finds more precious. And in the dusty streets, the noisy marketplaces and behind the doors of our city, every one of them trades in hopes, dreams and desires.

2 The Bargain Is Struck

With Durar's reprimand in my ears, I close my eyes and allow myself to remember how we have ended up here in this earthen house, which is crammed with paper and ink, and books bound in calfskin leather. Outside, I hear the bleating of goats being shepherded through the dusty streets, and the cries of traders, regaling each other with tales of far-flung places that I will never see.

Twenty years ago, when I first laid eyes on this place at the centre of the world, it was salt, not books, that kept its heart beating. Much has changed in my life, but little has altered in the life beyond my door. Heavy, grey slabs of rock salt, quarried three weeks journey northwards, and brought through the desert to Timbuktu by groaning, spitting teams of camels numbering over a thousand. Once they arrived, the Arab nomads who brought these trains, or *azalai*, sat on their haunches and waited for the dark-skinned traders from the south to cross the mighty Niger River, fifteen kilometres beyond.

At nightfall, across smouldering fires, travellers who truly did come from the ends of the earth sat across from each other, knowing that whoever spoke first would give away their position. In Timbuktu, it has been this way for generations, and so it will be for generations to come.

My uncle, Souma, had been one of those traders. For the last twelve years of his life and the first twelve of mine, he appeared in our village twice a year. The saddlebags on his donkeys were

alternately filled with gold as he headed first northwards to Timbuktu, then with salt as he journeyed back to the African towns that lay to the south. At that time, his world seemed full of mystery and adventure, while mine extended no further than a day's walk along the muddy paths that encircled my village.

Each year, we too engaged in bargaining, but in those days, it was I who was defeated at the outset. "Take me with you, Uncle," I would plead. I had not yet learnt to never speak first.

"And how would that grow my wealth or contentment?" he would reply. "You cannot bellow at a donkey, nor wield a dagger at the robbers who would steal my treasure, nor bargain with the wily desert Arabs. I should do nothing but worry about you the entire trip."

I remember my bargain and my uncle's response.

"I could boil millet porridge for you each morning and brush down the donkeys each evening," I said.

"No," said my uncle. He had sat beside too many smouldering fires to strike a bargain that would leave him with no profit.

A fly, sluggish and lazy with the midday heat, droned through my window and, in the distance, a stubborn camel brayed and groaned, protesting perhaps at the extra slab of salt that was loaded upon its back. But my mind was no longer in Timbuktu. I was once more at the start of my twelfth year, the year when everything changed.

That was the year of the locusts. They did not bargain. They simply swept out of the skies in great clouds that darkened the sun, taking whatever they wanted, giving nothing but hardship, hunger and desperation in return.

My uncle, who was far to the south, knew nothing of the plague that had visited us. But when he arrived from his six-monthly trek northwards, he was overcome by what he found.

Those of us who were still alive were gaunt from hunger, our eyes dulled from the hopelessness the onslaught of the locusts had brought. Our crops were ruined, our goats and cattle little more than ribs and skin.

I remember my uncle's expression as he led his donkeys into the village. I was sitting, wrapped up in a blanket, outside our hut. I stared into his eyes, saying nothing, and I can still remember the look of shock that came over his face when he finally recognised me.

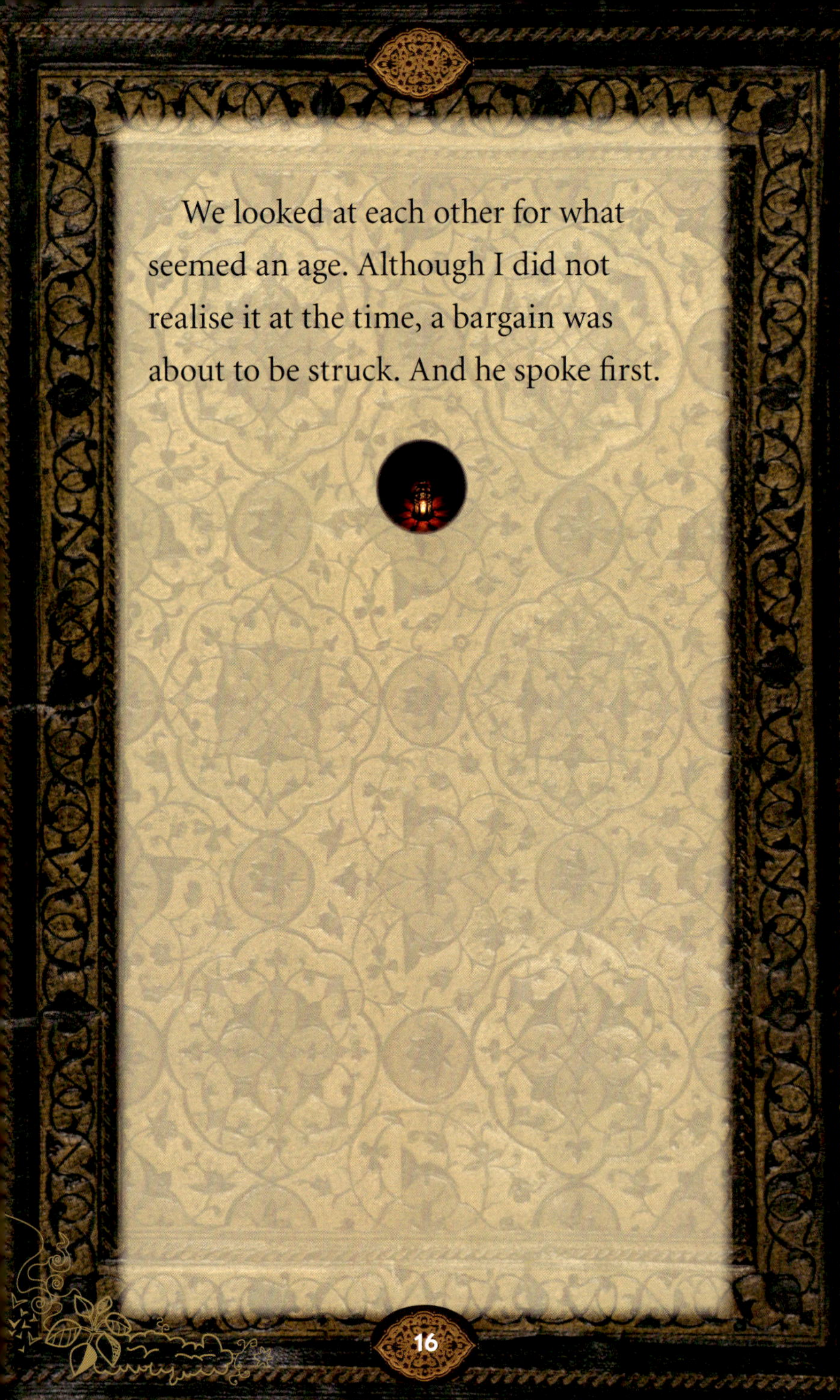

We looked at each other for what seemed an age. Although I did not realise it at the time, a bargain was about to be struck. And he spoke first.

3 The Price Is Paid

Sitting in my chair, my eyes closed, I remember it as clearly as if it were yesterday. When my uncle and I crossed the River Niger twenty years ago and my eyes first fell upon the city of Timbuktu, he turned to me and nodded. The deal was done.

It was a harsh bargain. Each of us ended up with what we had desired, although none of us felt richer for it. My parents, who had wished only that I should escape a time of hunger and deprivation, knew they were defeated at the outset. My uncle, who promised to sell me as a servant girl to an honest family, knew the gold he would receive would weigh heavily in his pockets and bring him no pleasure. I would get to see the mysterious place I had pleaded to visit for many years, but there would be no going back.

I marvelled at the strange pyramids that lined our path. Crowds of people dressed in flowing robes and with faces that marked a thousand different origins pushed past us. The relentless sun beat down upon us. Everywhere the smell of animals, people and the baking earth that had been beaten and shaped into a city rose and filled our nostrils. Finally, we stopped before a simple earthen house with a thatched roof.

The head of the Khalif family was Hasan, one of the scholars who had come to Timbuktu to learn from the teachers who taught at the three great schools of its university. He, in turn,

had become a teacher, and had settled, married and brought up a family. He was a quiet man who buried himself in the books that lined the rooms at the rear of the earthen house that I came to call home.

My uncle could not find it in his heart to bargain hard with Hasan's wife, Layla. She found the heat and the dust of Timbuktu oppressive and spent much of her day in her room, wishing she was back by the sapphire-blue waters of the Red Sea where she and Hasan had met. My duties there were simple: look after the three children; sweep out the sand that forced its way through every crack and crevice of the house; go to the market and prepare an evening meal for Hasan; and, three times a day, bring fresh tea to Layla and listen in silence while she told me of all she had given up to accompany her husband to this place she thought was at the end of the earth.

"There is nothing here but dirt and camel trains and wizened traders who squat in the street and argue and spit," she said. "Why did my husband trade our life of plenty, set between the glittering sea and the lush palms and grapevines, for this life of hardship? Does he really believe his books are more valuable than his wife's happiness?"

At first, I thought he did because, a year later, when Layla announced she and the children were leaving and going back to the sea, Hasan simply kissed her on the forehead and went to find consolation in his room full of books. It took me some years to realise that he had genuinely valued his wife's happiness, and he'd bought it for her by accepting the terrible price of years of loneliness for himself.

And so it was that I learned a lesson that served me well in the years since. The things that you value are not necessarily the things that others covet, and they will part with one to gain the other.

4 The Deal Is Done

After Hasan's wife and children left, my tasks diminished to merely sweeping sand and preparing an evening meal.

Sweep, shop and cook as I could, my duties did not extend to an entire day. And it wasn't long before I was drawn to my master's rooms at the rear of the house, curious as to the secret treasures that his rows of books held.

In the days before the locusts, I had snatched glimpses of the gold my uncle carried in his saddlebags. With its golden glow and heaviness, its ability to buy whatever goods one desired, I could understand its attraction. I had also seen the salt he carried south, and I understood its value to those who craved its taste and who used it

to preserve food for the times when the harvest and the hunting were scarce. But when I drew down the heavy volumes that lay stacked on the shelves, I saw nothing but paper, ink and leather. Like his wife before me, I could not see the value in these musty, yellowed tomes.

Three long, uneventful years of sweeping and preparing food passed, and I can remember little of that time.

The passage of time was slow in Timbuktu, marked only by more dirt and the cycle of camel trains arriving and departing with their treasures of heavy grey and gold.

Then one day, a little after I turned sixteen, there came a knock at the door. I put away my broom and drew back the bolt. There, in the dusty street, stood a tall man whose features marked him as one from the northwest.

"Is this the house of Hasan Khalif, the scholar and teacher?" he asked.

I nodded.

"Then I have something for him," said the man. He handed me a parcel, bound in rough papyrus.

"Hasan Khalif is not here," I said. "You must return tonight."

"I do not have time," said the man. "The Berbers I travel with are insisting on leaving Timbuktu before nightfall. This is a book that Hasan asked me to find for him. I have travelled throughout the lands of Arabia and beyond to bring it to him. You must give me eighty ducats now, or I shall leave."

I looked at the parcel. Eighty ducats? For a book? I handed the parcel back to the man.

"He already has plenty of books. Rows and rows of them. He will not want another."

"But this is a rare volume about the stars and the constellations!" protested the man. "Sixty ducats, and not a golden grain less!"

"No," I replied. The stars and the constellations that filled the clear skies above the desert were free for anyone to look at. What more could a book add?

"Forty ducats," insisted the man.

"I spend my days dusting the books Hasan Khalif already owns. I do not wish to add more books that will collect dust and cobwebs," I said, shaking my head.

"Twenty ducats," pleaded the man. "I have suffered greatly to satisfy Hasan's request, and now I shall barely make back the money I have paid the Berbers to bring me here."

I nodded at the man. The deal was done. I knew from his eyes that he would still leave here richer than when he arrived. I hoped that when my master came home, this book would also make him feel richer than when he left.

As I counted out the coins that my master kept hidden in a stone cooking jar, I hoped I'd made the right decision. Otherwise he would cast me out into the street and I would be left with nothing.

I paid the man and he turned to leave. He stopped and shook his head, looking at me with a wry expression. "Hasan Khalif has a shrewd wife," he said. "I doubt that even he, a learned scholar, could outsmart you."

I was about to correct his mistake but before I could, he hurried down the street in search of Berbers, camels and the new bargains that his twenty ducats might bring.

Sitting here alone, sixteen years later, in that very room, I have thought often of that moment. It has never failed to remind me how easily life can change.

5 The Debt Is Paid

"Twenty ducats?" roared Hasan. I was relieved to see his eyes sparkled with humour, not anger. "You managed to beat Ahmed the bookseller down to twenty ducats?" He stroked the leather binding of his new treasure and slowly turned the pages as if they were as fragile as life itself and the secrets they held as fleeting.

"I hope I have not negotiated a poor bargain, master," I said. "I was afraid I spent too much of your money."

"Nonsense. You have, in fact, saved me sixty ducats, for the first price he asked is exactly what I would have paid to have this book in my library."

"There is something else, master," I said hesitantly. "He thought I was your wife. I did not have time to correct him."

Hasan looked up from his book and I cast my eyes down to avoid his stare.

"I am sorry if this has caused you any shame," I murmured.

Hasan was silent for a moment longer, and then he gave an embarrassed laugh. "I should be so lucky," he said. "You cook and clean without a word of complaint, and you can get me the things I desire at a fraction of their true value. What better bargain could be struck?"

I stayed silent. Not because I didn't want to give my position away. I simply didn't know how to respond.

Another year passed. Like every preceding year, the same wizened traders disappeared and reappeared, filling their time between camel trains by squatting and arguing and spitting in Timbuktu's dry and dusty streets. Inside Hasan's house, the sand continued its daily invasion – but a change had come to our corner of Timbuktu. By the time Ahmed the bookseller returned that summer, I no longer had to correct his mistaken assumption.

It was a simple bargain. Hasan had paid off the debt of loneliness he had incurred for his first wife's happiness. He was prepared to incur another: the temporary disapproval of his neighbours and colleagues in order to secure something he valued above their approval. He told everyone that this thing was my ability to build his library by outwitting wily book traders. But I knew it was for something far simpler. Company.

In return, I asked only that he should be kind, look after me and teach me a little about the books in his rooms. If I had to spend my days dusting them, I should at least know why he insisted on collecting them. At the time, it may not have seemed like much of a bargain from my point of view – but sometimes the true value of a deal is not always apparent at its conclusion.

As time passed, I learned about books – what to look for and what to ignore. From time to time, Ahmed would come to our door, along with other book traders bringing their tightly bound treasures from the ends of the earth. I met with Hasan's colleagues, all of whom shared his passion for paper, ink and leather. I gradually became accepted as part of the rhythm that made Timbuktu the heart of the world. I learned that from this beating centre, veins and arteries carried not only yellow gold and slabs of grey rock salt, but an insatiable desire for learning and knowledge.

Soon it became known that instead of spending time trying to sell a hundred books to a hundred different scholars, a wise trader could instead negotiate one certain sale with one reliable customer. The rooms at the rear of the house became filled with books, from ceiling to floor, and the rooms at the front became filled with scholars, eager to swap ducats for knowledge. At sunset each evening, every one of us, traders, scholars and I, were richer in some way than we had been when the sun had risen that morning.

Ahmed, as the man who had inadvertently set me upon this path, slowly grew to become less of an adversary and more of a friend. In later years, he brought his son, Zaheen, with him.

"One day, I will be too old for all this travel," he groaned wearily. "I have brought Zaheen so he has years to get used to your shrewdness before he must fight for a ducat's profit on his own."

Ahmed always kept the most special books, the ones he had found in distant Persian bazaars or bartered from Moorish pirates, until last.

"Here is a treasure for you, Kella Khalif," he would say. "It's exquisite."

He would open its pages and point out the illuminations and decorations, hand-painted and finished with gold leaf and the dust of emeralds and rubies.

"I already have plenty of books. Rows and rows of them," I would say, smiling at Ahmed and recalling our first meeting. "I do not want another."

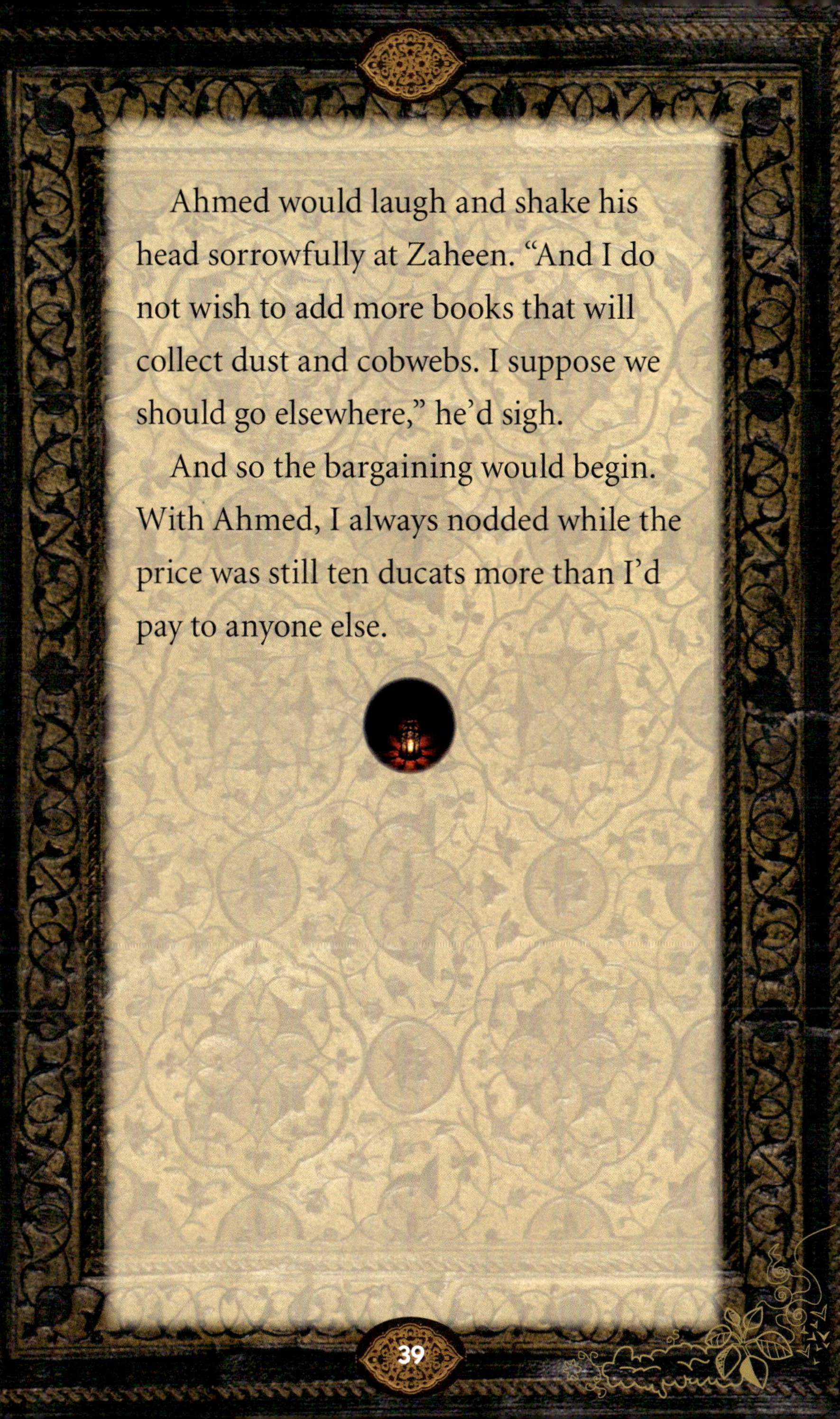

Ahmed would laugh and shake his head sorrowfully at Zaheen. "And I do not wish to add more books that will collect dust and cobwebs. I suppose we should go elsewhere," he'd sigh.

And so the bargaining would begin. With Ahmed, I always nodded while the price was still ten ducats more than I'd pay to anyone else.

6 What Price a Heart?

When my husband Hasan died, you might think that the bargain we had struck years earlier would come to an end. But, as I have said, the true value of a deal is not always apparent at its conclusion.

For, while I had learned the value that scholars place upon the things they desire, the books and the gold that they brought to our household were not the things that left me feeling richer than when we had nodded and sealed our bargain. The true treasure that we secured was not brought through a desert on the back of a dusty camel, nor carried across the River Niger in a donkey's pack. It was born to us on a rainy, windy day when the dusts of the desert from the north and the clouds of the jungles to the south collided in the skies of Timbuktu. Her name was Durar.

Here, at the very heart of the world, is a city where people have always come and gone, but always the rhythm of life continues. The camel trains bring grey slabs of salt and the donkeys bring packs of yellow gold, as they have for a thousand years, and will for a thousand more. Only the faces of the traders bargaining in the streets change. And so it is with Durar and me.

Ismail, who has just left with his prized book, has only been at the schools of the great university for a few years. Durar is only twelve, the age that I was when I first laid my eyes upon the city I now call home. One day, she will sit here instead of me, receiving scholars and book traders. And one of those traders will be Ahmed's son, Zaheen. Indeed, it was he who brought me the book I have just sold to Ismail, along with the one I will sell to el-Shabeni tomorrow.

I open my eyes once more, and the world of the present floods back. I sigh. Enough of the past. It is gone forever, and its joys and sorrows are as fleeting as the wisps of cloud that gather beyond our reach, high in the blue desert skies.

I have other things on my mind. Ahmed, who rarely makes the long journey to Timbuktu these days, was right about me the first day we met. I am shrewd. Shrewd enough to see the way that Durar looks at Zaheen when he knocks at our door, and shrewd enough to see that, sooner or later, he will return those glances and there will come a day when it will be me who is defeated before I start.

Outside, the salt traders and gold merchants will argue, haggle and eye each other sorrowfully over the embers of smouldering fires, and deals will be done. But here, inside this room, on that day, there will be more than a simple bargain to be struck.

I imagine Durar and Zaheen will sit before me, and for the first time in my life, I will wonder what could possibly be half as precious as the thing I am about to give up. Zaheen had better be prepared to bargain hard before I nod and we leave this room with the things that we all desire.

Not gold, nor salt nor books. Nothing, in fact, that can be brought from the ends of the earth. Only that which can be found in its heart. I sigh and stand. That day will come. In the meantime, there are books to sell.

At the Heart of the World

Author's Note

The Islamic University of Timbuktu was a respected centre of teaching and learning in medieval times. Over hundreds of years, countless manuscripts were collected there. Timbuktu is now little more than an impoverished town in the northern provinces of the African state of Mali, surviving mainly from the salt trade, which still continues. Many of the ancient manuscripts and books collected by the medieval scholars survived, passed down through families who lived in Timbuktu, or buried for years in cellars and hidden between the walls of the old mosques scattered throughout the town.

These manuscripts and books, many of which are in poor condition and in danger of decaying, now form the collection of several libraries in Timbuktu, holding up to 700 000 written treasures. Some of them date from the thirteenth century and most are irreplaceable.

In the last decade, two Timbuktu manuscripts projects funded by universities in Europe and South Africa have aimed to preserve them. Unfortunately, many of the poorer families who hold manuscripts sell them for desperately needed money – in some reported cases, for as little as $50 each.

It seems that even today, people still meet in Timbuktu, each of them possessing something that someone else desires.

But, as our storyteller might say, the deals that people are forced to make in Timbuktu now are not good bargains to strike. The loss of these medieval treasures leave no one richer, and all of us poorer.

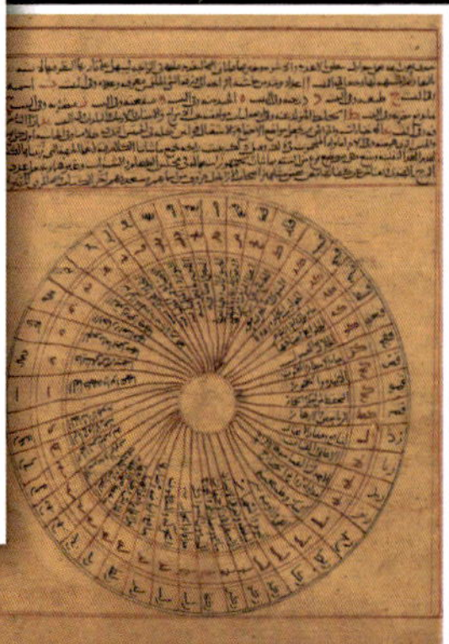

rare Arabic manuscripts from Timbuktu